**For all my friends.**
**D.T.**

**In memory of Harry – a fantastic friend to so many.**
**And to Asha and the three little Mootoos – Taryn, Nate and Reyan.**
**With much love, L.S. xx**

First published in Great Britain in 2018 by Boxer Books Limited.
www.boxerbooks.com

Boxer® is a registered trademark of Boxer Books Limited.

Text copyright © 2018 Leilani Sparrow • Illustrations copyright © 2018 Dan Taylor

The illustrations were prepared digitally by the illustrator.
The text is set in Futura PT

ISBN 978-1-910716-25-0

1 3 5 7 9 10 8 6 4 2

Manufactured in Malaysia

All of our papers are sourced from managed forests and renewable resources.

# My Best Friends

by Leilani Sparrow

Illustrated by Dan Taylor

Boxer Books

# It's fun to find an old friend.

It's great to make
a new friend.

When you're sick in bed,
I'm a feel-better-soon
friend.

On special days I have
party friends.

# I made a sad friend.

I'm sorry, we make up,
and now I have
a glad friend.

In the rain I see

a wet friend.

I share and make
dry friends.

I love camping with
my best friends.

At school I have my
class friends.

# At home I have my pet friends.

**But most of all,
at work or play,
all my friends
are best friends.**